USBORNE FIRST READING
Level Two

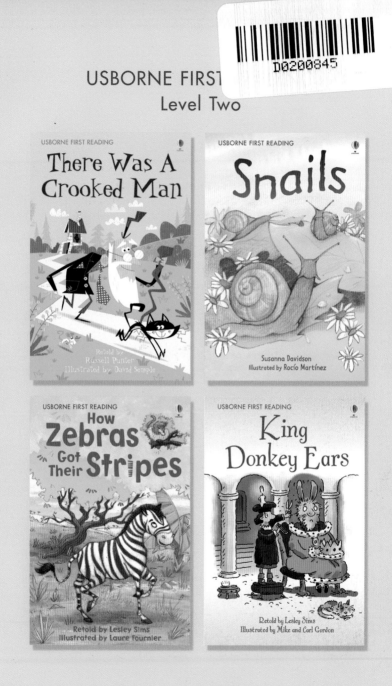

USBORNE FIRST READING

There Was A Crooked Man

Retold by Russell Punter
Illustrated by David Semple

USBORNE FIRST READING

Snails

Susanna Davidson
Illustrated by Rocío Martínez

USBORNE FIRST READING

How Zebras Got Their Stripes

Retold by Lesley Sims
Illustrated by Laure Fournier

USBORNE FIRST READING

King Donkey Ears

Retold by Lesley Sims
Illustrated by Mike and Carl Gordon

One, Two, Buckle My Shoe

Retold by Russell Punter

Illustrated by David Semple

Reading consultant: Alison Kelly
Roehampton University

One, two,

buckle my shoe.

Three, four,

knock at the door.

Five, six,

pick up sticks.

Seven, eight,

lay them straight.

Nine, ten,

Gertie

a big fat hen.

Eleven, twelve,

dig and delve.

Thirteen, fourteen,

maids a-courting.

Fifteen, sixteen,

maids in the kitchen.

Seventeen, eighteen,

maids a-waiting.

Nineteen, twenty,
my plate's empty.

Twenty-one, twenty-two,
"Shoo fox, shoo!"

Twenty-three,
twenty-four,

home once more.

Twenty-five, twenty-six,

"Let's get this fixed."

Twenty-seven,
twenty-eight,

fasten the gate.

Twenty-nine, thirty,

Gertie

"You're safe now,
Gertie."

PUZZLES
Puzzle 1
Can you spot the differences between these two pictures? There are six to find.

Puzzle 2

Choose the best phrase for each picture.

1.

A-Tickle my shoe.

B-Buckle my shoe.

2.

A-A big fat hen.

B-A big fat pen.

Puzzle 3
Put the pictures in order.

A

B

C

D

E

F

Answers to puzzles

Puzzle 1

Puzzle 2

1.

B-Buckle my shoe.

2.

A-A big fat hen.

Puzzle 3

1. D

2. B

3. A

4. F

5. C

6. E

One, Two, Buckle My Shoe is a traditional number rhyme with many variations. It usually ends at the number twenty, but this version has been extended to thirty.

Series editor: Lesley Sims

First published in 2010 by Usborne Publishing Ltd., Usborne House, 83-85 Saffron Hill, London EC1N 8RT, England. www.usborne.com
Copyright © 2010 Usborne Publishing Ltd.

USBORNE FIRST READING
Level Three

USBORNE FIRST READING

Dinosaurs

Conrad Mason
Illustrated by
Daniel Howarth

USBORNE FIRST READING

The Magic Pear Tree

Retold by
Rosie Dickins

Illustrated by
Matt Ward

USBORNE FIRST READING

The Peach Boy

Retold by
Alex Frith
Illustrated by
Kelly Murphy

USBORNE FIRST READING

The Old Woman who swallowed a Fly

Illustrated by
Sarah Horne